D1006485

Finn & Jake's Awesome Activities on the Go!

by Jake Black

illustrated by
Stephen Reed

PSS!
PRICE STERN SLOAN
An Imprint of Penguin Group (USA) Inc.

PRICE STERN SLOAN
Published by the Penguin Group
Penguin Group (USA) Inc., 375 Hudson Street, New York, New York 10014, USA
Penguin Group (Canada), 90 Eglinton Avenue East, Suite 700, Toronto, Ontario M4P 2Y3, Canad
(a division of Pearson Penguin Canada Inc.)
Penguin Books Ltd, 80 Strand, London WC2R ORL, England
Penguin Ireland, 25 St Stephen's Green, Dublin 2, Ireland (a division of Penguin Books Ltd)
Penguin Group (Australia), 707 Collins Street, Melbourne, Victoria 3008, Australia
(a division of Pearson Australia Group Pty Ltd)
Penguin Books India Pvt Ltd, 11 Community Centre, Panchsheel Park, New Delhi—110 017, India
Penguin Group (NZ), 67 Apollo Drive, Rosedale, Auckland 0632, New Zealand
(a division of Pearson New Zealand Ltd)
Penguin Books, Rosebank Office Park, 181 Jan Smuts Avenue, Parktown North 2193, South Afric
Penguin China, B7 Jaiming Center, 27 East Third Ring Road North,
Chaoyang District, Beijing 100020, China

Penguin Books Ltd, Registered Offices: 80 Strand, London WC2R ORL, England

All rights reserved. No part of this book may be reproduced, scanned, or distributed in any printed or electronic form without permission. Please do not participate in or encourage piracy of copyrighted materials in violation of the author's rights. Purchase only authorized editions.

The publisher does not have any control over and does not assume any responsibility for author or third-party websites or their content.

ADVENTURE TIME, CARTOON NETWORK, the logos, and all related characters and elements are trademarks of and © Cartoon Network. (s13)

Published in 2013 by Price Stern Sloan, a division of Penguin Young Readers Group,
345 Hudson Street, New York, New York 10014.
PSS! is a registered trademark of Penguin Group (USA) Inc.
Printed in the U.S.A.

ISBN 978-0-8431-7341-3

10 9 8 7 6 5 4 3 2

ALWAYS LEARNING

PEARSON

Welcome from Finn

Map of Ooo

All of our adventures happen here in the Land of Ooo.
What are your favorite places in the Land of Ooo?
Circle 'em, and make sure to visit them while you're here!
N
W
S

THE LAND OF
OOO
FOREST
THE SEA OF SOMETHING
THE UNKNOWN LANDS
THE SHINY ISLES
THE CAVES
ROCK CANDY MOUNTAINS
ICE KINGDOM
MOUNTAIN KINGDOM
CANDY KINGDOM
GRASS LANDS
HAUNTED SWAMP
THE HOLE NEAR THE CENTER OF THE WORLD
LOST CLIFFS
KINGDOM OF FIRE
DESERT LANDS
ISLE OF STEAM
BAD LANDS
CHICKEN BLOOD COVE

Witch Dots?

Oh man! Jake was turned invisible by the Witch! Connect the dots to help him reappear! When you're done, color him, so I can see him!

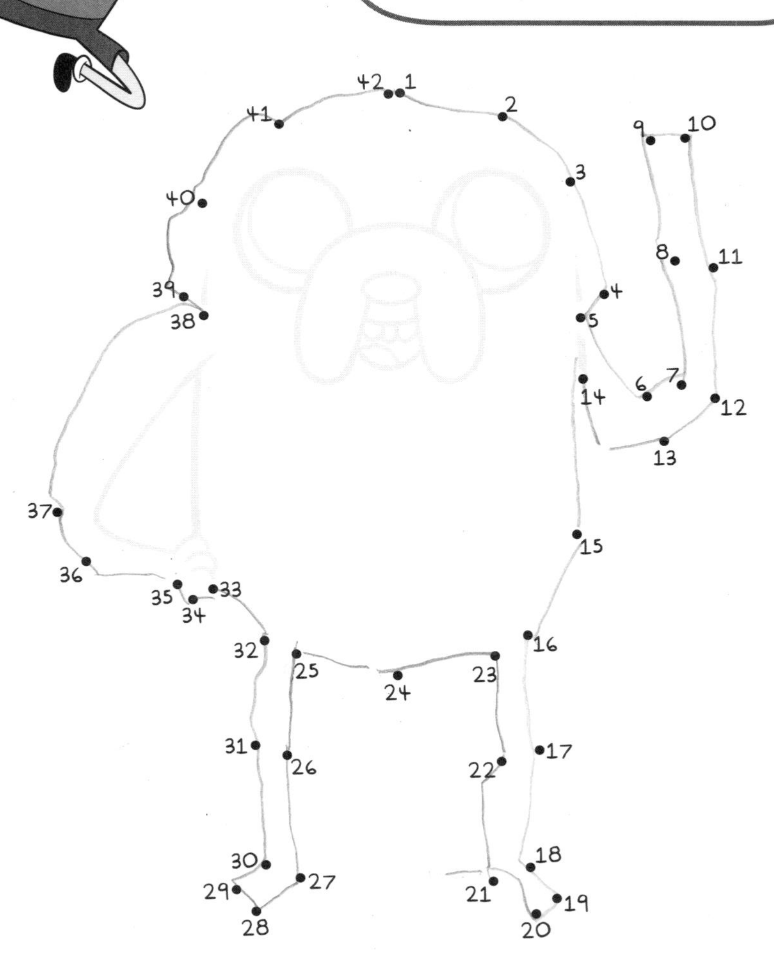

Coded Message

Jake left Finn a coded message. Use the key below to break the code. Write Jake's message in the space provided.

"YZW YRHXFRGH NZPV GSV YZPVI YILPV, YIL!"

Code

A = Z	J = Q	S = H
B = Y	K = P	T = G
C = X	L = O	U = F
D = W	M = N	V = E
E = V	N = M	W = D
F = U	O = L	X = C
G = T	P = K	Y = B
H = S	Q = J	Z = A
I = R	R = I	

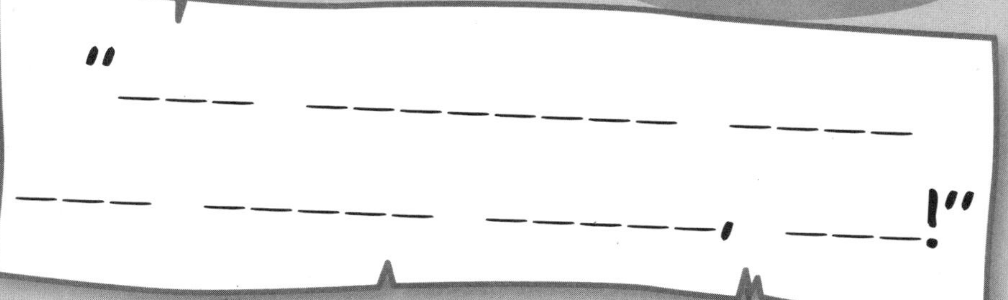

Scrambled Names

Some totally righteous and wrongteous peeps live in the Land of Ooo. Unscramble their names.

1. RPICNESS EBBBULGMU

2. JKAE

3. NFIN

4. CIE GKIN

5. MRAELCNIE

6. ADLY IRARICNON

7. OBM

A-Maze-Ing Adventure

What's the Difference?

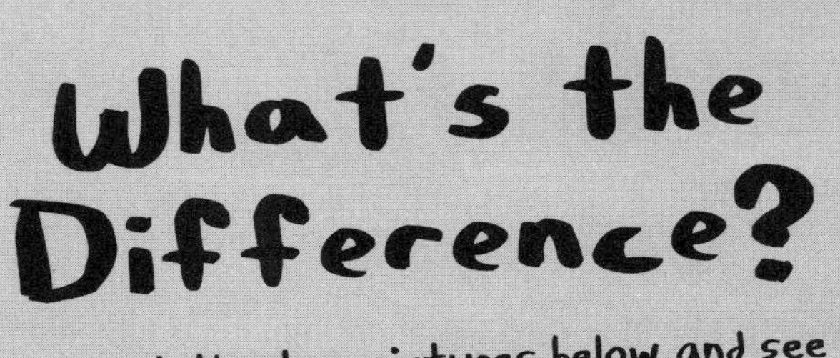

Check out the two pictures below and see if you can spot ten differences between them.

Attack of the Candy Zombies!

Candy Zombies are attacking the Candy Kingdom! Draw what you think Candy Zombies look like in the space below!

How Do I Look?

How well do you know the Adventure Time crew? Check out the extreme close-ups of your favorite characters. Draw a line between the pictures and characters that match.

Finn

Jake

Princess Bubblegum

BMO

Ice King

What Are You Talking About?!

Jake and Finn need to make a plan before they go into battle against the Ice King. What do you think they should do? Use the space below to write out their plans.

Searching for Words

Here's a word search. It's got everybody's names in it. Can you find them all? Don't forget to look diagonally and backward.

F N R E T B U B B L E G U M M
N O L Y R L A P N P W U M Z A
C K S S H U M R A H K N Z R R
N I S G R O T Z H K U T F G C
X K E W D O T N F I L E V U E
M W C G P R N J E S N R T W L
W G N T J N R W H V S X L E I
S I I H A D O M F G D D J Z N
K V R E K M C V I N Y A J T E
T D P W E R I D O I J I U S Y
F S H M Q N N H N K F B M O Y
G I U D W L I V N E Y I H G B
G H N Q A T A D A C A T B E P
L Z U N S E R Z D I A C A K E
M R C A N D Y H D A R Q T K F

ADVENTURE
BMO
BUBBLEGUM
CAKE
CANDY
FINN
FIONNA
GUNTER
ICE KING
JAKE
KINGDOM
MARCELINE
ME-MOW
PRINCESS
RAINICORN

Cross Words

Don't argue with your friends. Get it? Having cross words? No? Don't think that's funny? Well, just see if you can fill in the answers to this crossword puzzle.

ACROSS

1. Place where adventures happen
4. Greatest adventurer in the history of the world
6. Princess who Finn is in love with
7. Jake's girlfriend
8. Dog with special powers

DOWN

2. What time is it?
3. Rock star vampire
5. Finn and Jake's archenemy

In the Shadows

The Witches have cast a dark spell over the Candy Kingdom, turning everyone into shadows! Can you figure out who each shadow really is? Write the name under the shadow below!

Princess Bubblegum
Finn
Marceline
Ice King
Jake

Squaring Off in the Battlefield

Squaring off means facing your enemy on the battlefield. A true adventurer always squares off bravely. Play this game with a friend. Each player takes a turn connecting the dots, one line at a time, to make a square. (The lines should only be horizontal and vertical, not diagonal.) When you complete the square, put your initials in it. Then you get to take another turn. You can use your opponent's lines to make squares. Once all the squares have been made, the player with the most wins the game.

Memory Test
Study this picture of a great adventure carefully. Then turn the page.

BMO

Memory Test (continued)

See how many questions you can answer correctly without peeking at the picture on the previous page.

1. Who are Finn and Jake fighting?

2. How many characters are there?

3. Is Finn's mouth open or closed?

4. How many legs is Jake standing on?

5. In which hand is Finn holding his weapon?

6. What weapon is Finn using?

7. What is in Finn's other hand?

8. How many good guys are there?

9. Who is falling backward?

10. How many bolts of magic are there?

Join the Adventure!

Finn and Jake want you to join them in the Land of Ooo and be a great warrior. You can fight alongside them and conquer the evil Ice King, Candy Zombies, and whoever else threatens the Candy Kingdom with their evil acts. Just draw a picture of yourself below, and you're in!

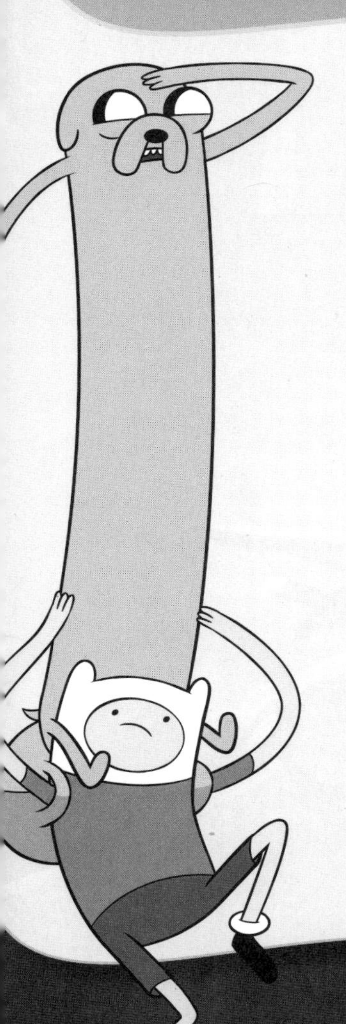

One of These Things Is Not Like the Others

Jake loves posing in front of a mirror to see how totally awesome his powers make him look. Look at the pictures below and figure out which is different from the rest.

Guess Who?

Use the clues to guess this mystery character.
Write your answer in the space below.

1. I love going on adventures!
2. I have special powers that let me twist and stretch my body in weird ways.
3. I am in love with Lady Rainicorn.
4. My best friend is Finn.
5. I'm not human.

Rescue the Princess

Princess Bubblegum has been captured by the Ice King. To save her, play this game with a friend, using pennies as game pieces. Place your pennies on Start with Jake and Finn. Take turns moving around the game board. On your turn, flip a coin—move ahead two spaces for heads and one space for tails. The first player to make it to the Ice King's castle wins.

18
19
20
21
17
Rockin' out with Marceline. Jump ahead one space.
23
Tricked by Me-Mow. Go back three spaces.
22
Conquered a game on BMO. Jump ahead two spaces.
BMO
16
24
25
15
26
14
27
You made it! You saved Princess Bubblegum from the clutches of the evil Ice King! You win!
13
Knife storm! Go back one space.

Adventure Time Bingo

Next time you watch *Adventure Time*, pay close attention to everything that happens and everything that's said. When you see or hear one of the pictures on the bingo board below, cover it with a small piece of paper. When you cover an entire line, yell out "Bingo." You're the winner!

Team Up

Adventures are always better when you have a partner to team up with. You can make up teams by drawing a line from the character on the left to their partner on the right. Will these teams work together? Or will they totally implode in disaster? There are no right answers, so have fun imagining the adventures these teams could have together.

Coded Message #2

We've received another coded message! Help us save the day by using the code to break it!

"Zodzbh yv irtsgvlfh!"

Code

	I = R	R = I
A = Z	J = Q	S = H
B = Y	K = P	T = G
C = X	L = O	U = F
D = W	M = N	V = E
E = V	N = M	W = D
F = U	O = L	X = C
G = T	P = K	Y = B
H = S	Q = J	Z = A

"_______ __

__________!"

Lost in the Maze

Finn and Jake are lost in a maze of trees and bushes! Help them find their way out!

Logic Puzzle

The creatures in the Land of Ooo look like animals and objects from our world but are just a little bit different (for example, they talk!). Can you figure out which animal or object is a creature in the Candy Kingdom? Read the clues, and mark the correct answer in the grid below.

	VIDEO GAME SYSTEM	DOG	UNICORN	HEART
JAKE				
LADY RAINICORN				
RICARDIO				
BMO				

Who Am I?

Answer the clues to discover the mystery character. Write your answer in the space below.

1. I'm more than one thousand years old.
2. I love rocking out with a guitar.
3. I am a vampire queen.
4. I can turn into monsterlike shapes.
5. Sometimes I help Finn and Jake in their adventures.

More of What's the Difference?

Check out the two pictures below and see if you can spot ten differences between them.

Adventure Story Time!

Here are several scenes from an adventure Jake and Finn had together. In the space provided below each picture, write the story of this great adventure!

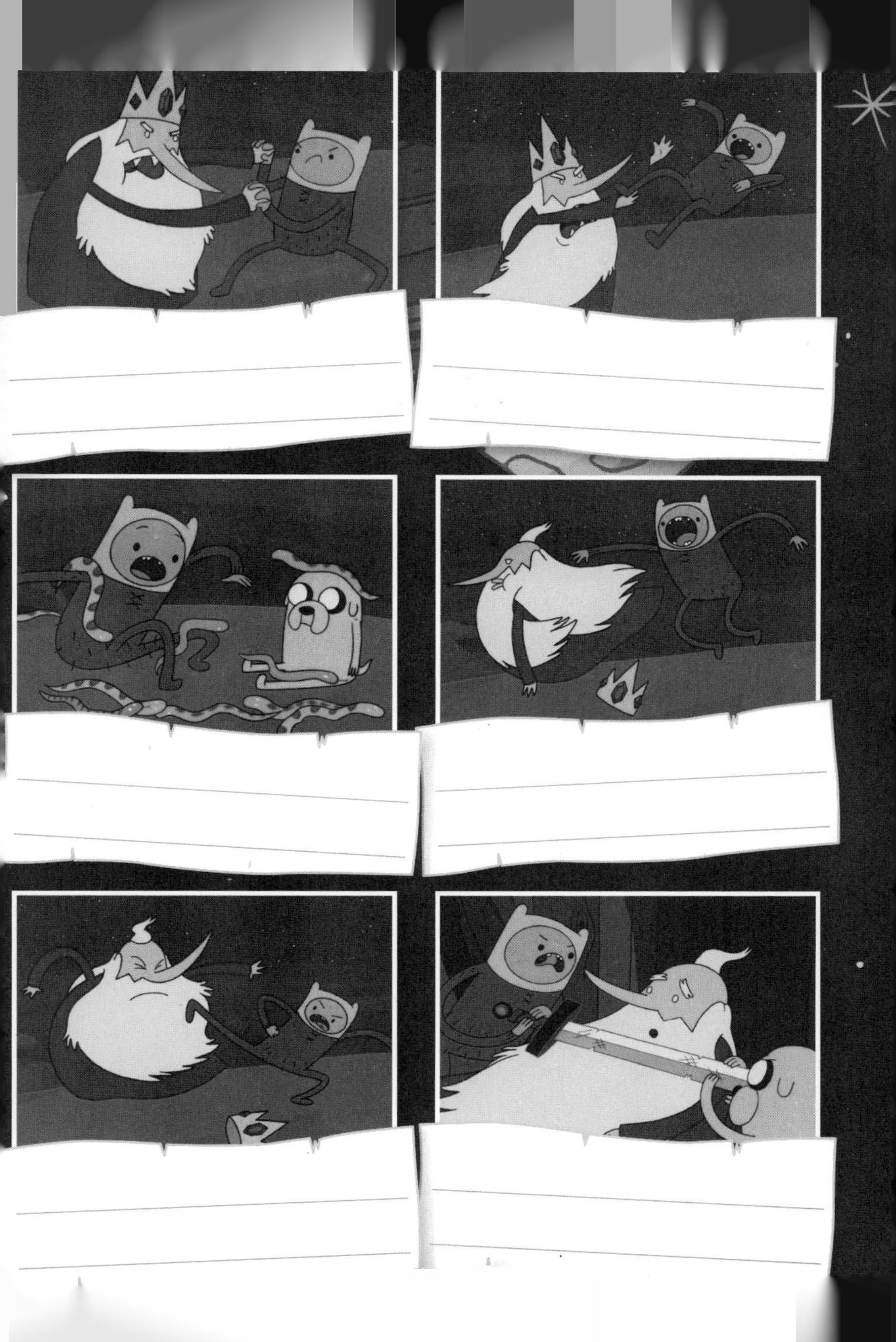

Guitar Star

Marceline desperately wants a new guitar. In the space below, draw the wickedest, most kick-butt guitar the world has ever seen!

Create Your Own Adventure Time Adventure (Part One)

Have you ever wanted to create your own *Adventure Time* adventures? Using safety scissors (and help from an adult), cut out the characters here and on the next page, and place them on the map at the front of this book. Then play out your very own *Adventure Time* adventures!

Create Your Own Adventure Time Adventure (Part Two)

Daddy Dots

Marceline's daddy is one creepy dude. He has crazy powers like Marceline. Connect the dots to make him appear out of nowhere!

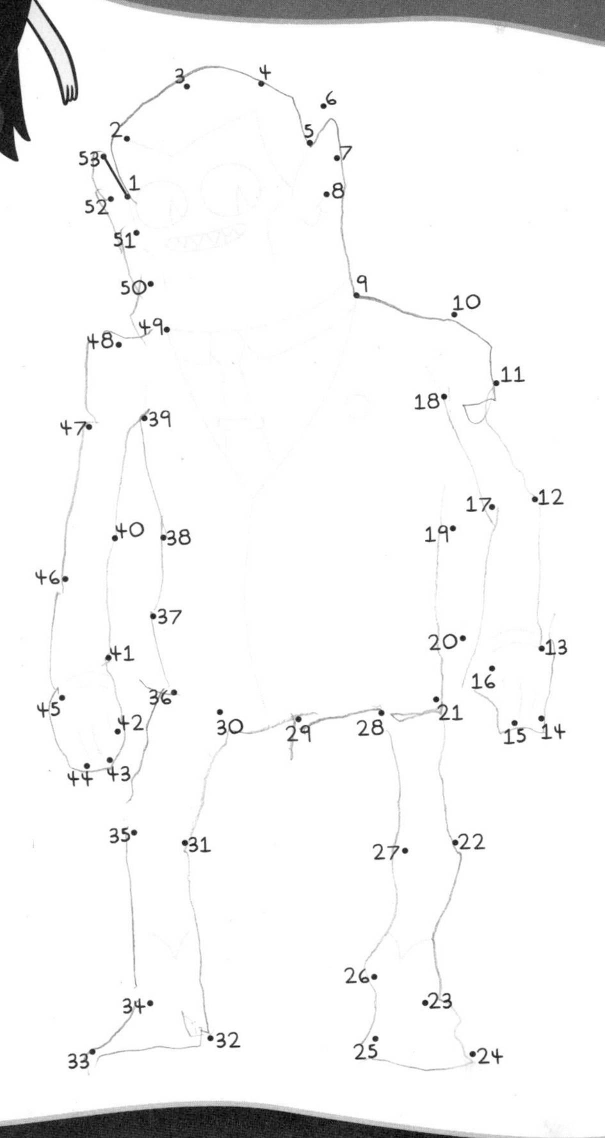

Game Time

BMO is Finn and Jake's friend. It's an alarm clock, a camera, and of course, a video game player. In fact, Jake and Finn are playing a video game right now! They just need you to draw it on BMO's screen below! Better make it exciting. They don't want to play lame, boring games!

Sweet Sudoku

A sudoku puzzle consists of a grid with nine squares across and nine squares down. The grid is broken up into nine three-by-three boxes. The object is to fill in the empty squares with numbers, so that every nine-box row and nine-box column contains each of the numbers from one to nine. Every three-by-three box should also contain each number from one to nine. No row, column, or box should have the same number included twice.

Now, check out the number code below for your favorite characters, and find where each number goes on the grid.

1. Finn
2. Jake
3. Marceline
4. BMO
5. Ice King
6. Princess Bubblegum
7. Lady Rainicorn
8. Lumpy Space Princess
9. Tree Trunks

How to Draw: Finn

Below are step-by-step instructions for how to draw Finn from *Adventure Time*! Follow the steps to draw him yourself!

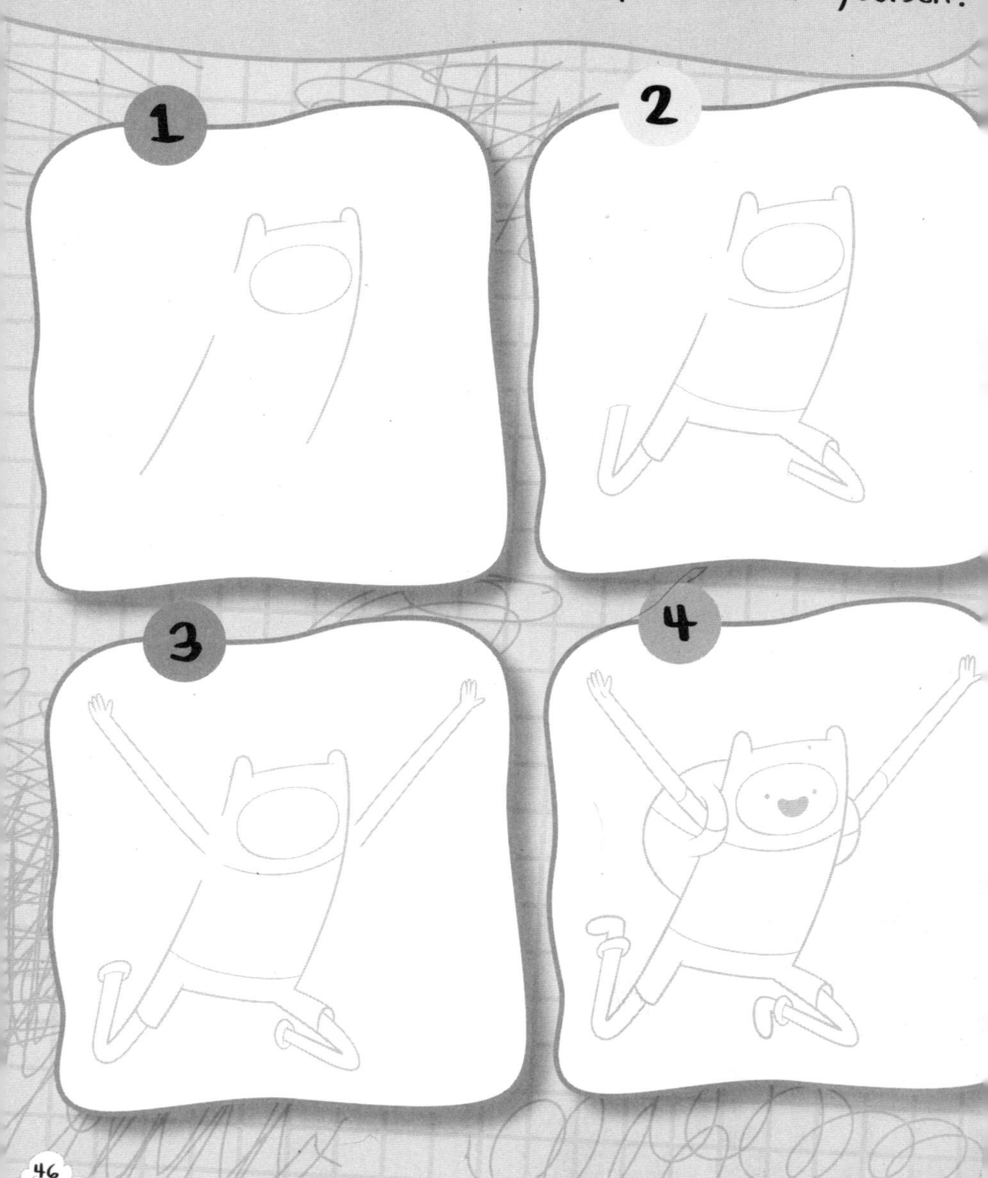

Parental Units

Draw a line from the characters to their parents.

Marceline

Joshua

Jake

Lumpy Space King

Lady Rainicorn

Hunson Abadeer

Lumpy Space Princess

Bob

Tree Fort Door Hanger

Do you ever need to get away to your secret Tree Fort? With the help of a parent (and safety scissors), cut out this door hanger and put it on your favorite doorknob. It will tell everyone you need to be left alone to plan your next adventure!

KEEP OUT!
TREE FORT!

Candy House

If you lived in the Candy Kingdom in the Land of Ooo, what would your house look like? Would it be a castle like Princess Bubblegum's or a house like Jake and Finn's? Draw it below!

Changing Images

Sometimes things aren't always as they appear. Look at the six pictures of Finn below. Figure out which one is different from the rest.

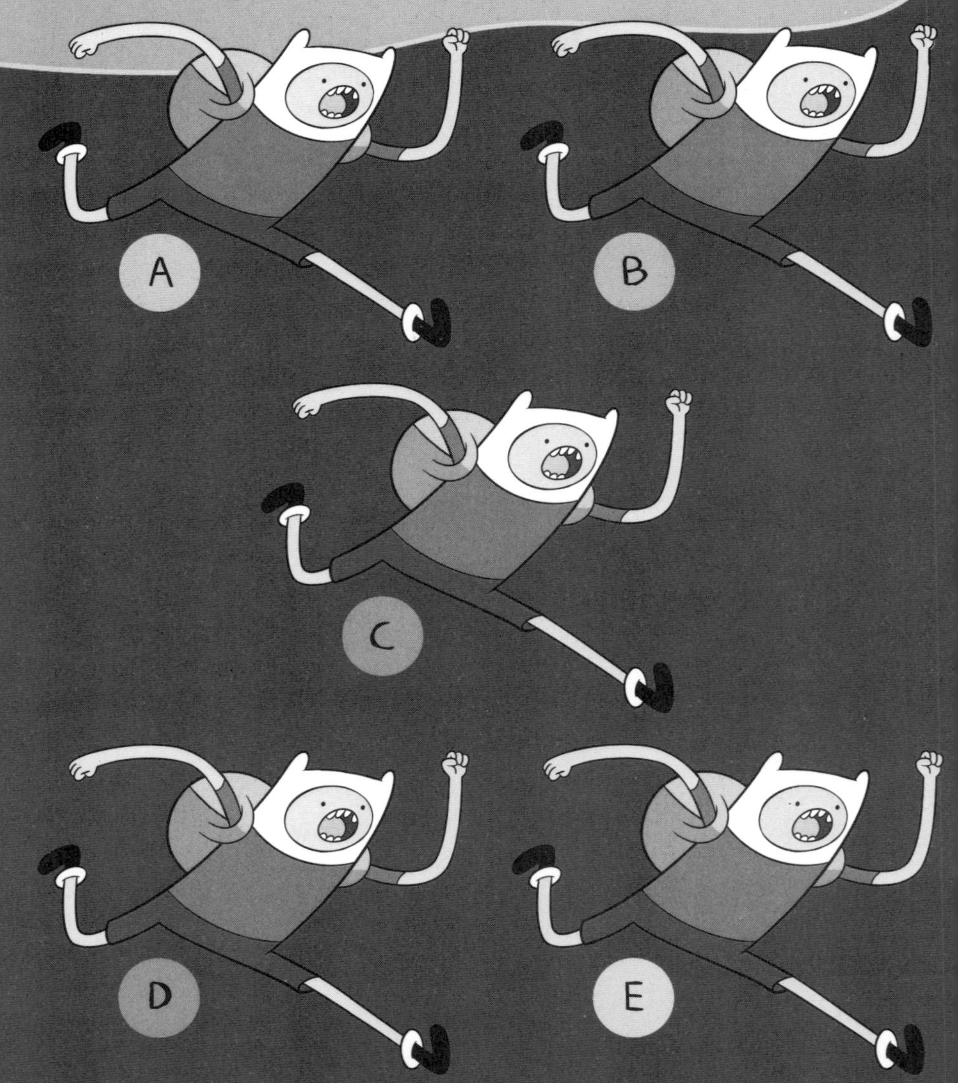

Squiggle Maze

Jake's arms and legs can stretch out really long, and twist and turn in all sorts of directions. Follow each of his arms and legs, and figure out what they're grabbing!

Hide and Seek

Find Jake and Finn in the picture below.
Circle them when you find them.

Sing, Marceline, Sing

Marceline is singing an awesome song! Write the words to the song in the space provided. (Remember, they should rhyme!)

Words!

How many words can you make using the letters found in *ADVENTURE TIME*? Write them in the space below. You can even challenge your friends to see how many they can find.

The Final Battle

Draw the biggest battle adventure in the history of the world! It should be epic. It should be totally awesome. It should be . . . well, you get the idea.

Answers

Page 6

Witch Dots?

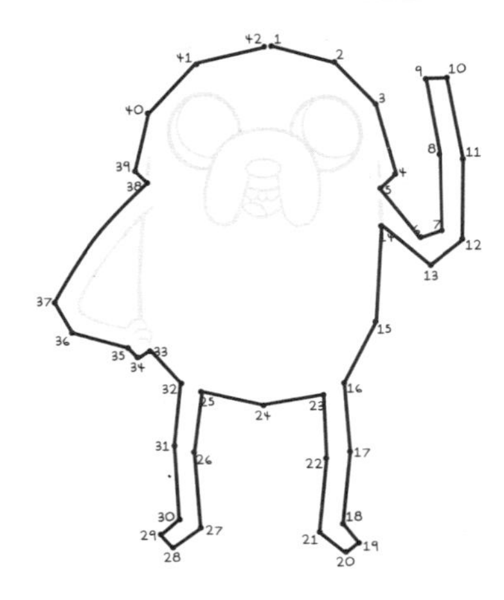

Page 7

Coded Message

"BAD BISCUITS MAKE THE BAKER BROKE, BRO!"

Page 8

Scrambled Names

1. Princess Bubblegum
2. Jake
3. Finn
4. Ice King
5. Marceline
6. Lady Rainicorn
7. BMO

Page 9

A-Maze-Ing Adventure

Pages 10–11

What's the Difference?

Page 13

How Do I Look?

1. BMO, 2. Ice King, 3. Jake, 4. Finn, 5. Princess Bubblegum

Page 16

Searching for Words

F N R E T B U B B L E G U M M
N O L Y R L A P N P W U M Z A
C K S S H U M R A H K N Z R R
N I S G R O T Z H K U T F G C
X K E W D O T N F I L E V U E
M W C G P R N J E S N R T W L
W G N T J N R W H V S X L E I
S I I H A D O M F G D D J Z N
K V R E K M C V I N Y A J T E
T D P W E R I D O I J I U S Y
F S H M Q N N H N K F B M O Y
G I U D W L I V N E Y I H G B
G H N Q A T A D A C A T B E P
L Z U N S E R Z D I A C A K E
M R C A N D Y H D A R Q T K F

Page 17

Cross Words

Page 18

In the Shadows

1. Finn
2. Jake
3. Princess Bubblegum
4. Marceline
5. Ice King

Page 22

Memory Test

1. The Ice King
2. 6
3. open
4. 4
5. his right
6. sword
7. shield
8. 5
9. BMO
10. 2

Page 24

One of These Things Is Not Like the Others

Jake is missing his tail in picture C

Page 25

Guess Who?

Jake

Page 30

Coded Message #2

"Always be righteous!"

Page 31

Lost in the Maze

Page 32

Logic Puzzle

	VIDEO GAME SYSTEM	DOG	UNICORN	HEART
JAKE		X		
LADY RAINICORN			X	
RICARDIO				X
BMO	X			

Page 33

Who Am I?

Marceline

Pages 34-35

More of What's the Difference?

Page 43

Daddy Dots

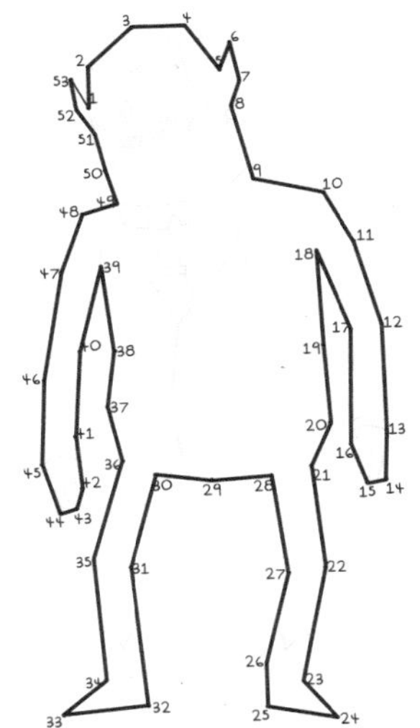

Page 45

Sweet Sudoku

Page 48

Parental Units

Marceline - Hunson Abadeer
Jake - Joshua
Lady Rainicorn - Bob
Lumpy Space Princess - Lumpy Space King

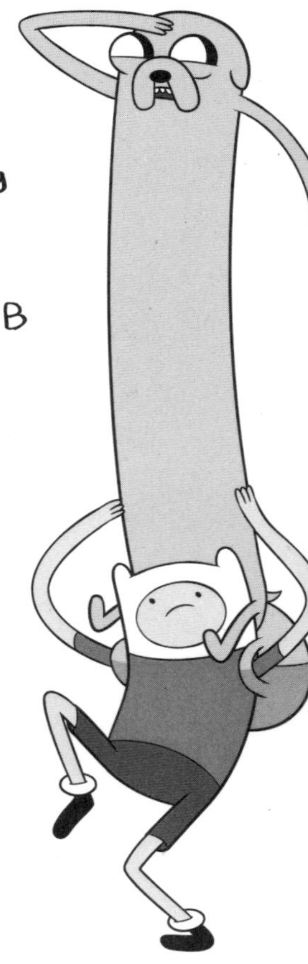

Page 52

Changing Images

Finn's shoulder strap is missing in picture B

Page 53

Squiggle Maze

A-3, B-4, C-1, D-2

Pages 54–55

Hide and Seek